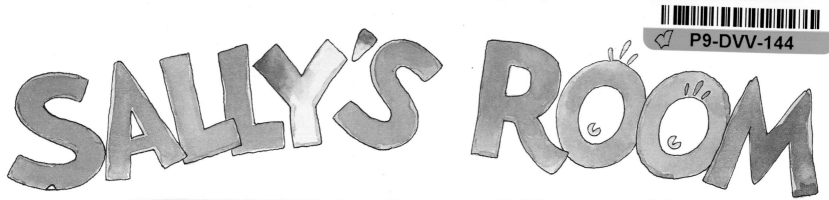

SALLY'S ROOM

M.K. BROWN

Scholastic Inc.

NEW YORK TORONTO LONDON AUCKLAND SYDNEY

Dedicated to
Tessa Brunton,
Sarah Oleson, Sophie Priola,
Lindsey Reidy, Shannon Reidy,
Marla Solberg, Mary Sutliff,
and Sarah Vincent.

And to my daughter,
Kalia Kliban,
who inspired this book.

ISBN 0-590-44710-6

Copyright © 1992 by M.K. Brown.
All rights reserved. Published by Scholastic Inc.

12 11 10 9 8 7 6 5 4 3 2   2 3 4 5 6 7/9

Printed in the U.S.A.   08

Designed by M.K. Brown and
Claire Counihan

The artwork was painted in watercolor
with India ink linework.

Late one morning as Sally got ready for school,
she stepped on a stegosaurus, then she stepped on a triceratops.
She couldn't find her colored pencils, and she couldn't
find her favorite sweater.

Sally left the house that morning in a very bad mood.

Sally's room was in a bad mood, too.
The lamp spoke up.
"What are you laughing at?"
It glared at the globe.

"You've got socks on your head,
ha, ha," explained the globe.

"You've both got socks
on your heads," said a
clock with no batteries.

"Never mind that!" yelled a chair. "Look at me! Who could sit on me? I'm stuffed! I'm going under!"

"Ick," said a fishbowl that badly needed scrubbing.

"Yuck," said half a peanut butter sandwich.

"That's nothing," said the bureau. "Just look at that bed!"

Everybody looked at the bed. Now the bed began to squirm.

"What's wrong with me? I'm very comfortable the way I am, sort of," said the bed.

Some checkers fell out. An almost complete jigsaw puzzle fell out.

"How can you possibly be comfortable," they yelled, "with crayons and dinosaurs and scratchy doll clothes all mixed up in your sheets?"

"Come to think of it," the bed said, "I could use a little house cleaning."

"We all could," stated the globe.

"Exactly," said the clock. "It is time for a change!"

"Let's go find Sally right now!" they all shouted. "Let's tell her just how we feel!"

Sally's messy room marched out the door and down the street,
through the center of town, past the corner market,
past the library, past the fire station,
and up the long driveway to school.

People almost fainted
when they saw it.
Even dogs and cats
ran away fast.

At the school, the custodian got excited and fell into a bush.
The principal screamed.

Squeezing through the front door was not easy.
But Sally's room was determined.
It got in.
Down the hall and up the stairs it went, looking for Sally.

The teacher, Mrs. Locati, had just asked the class, "What is the capital of Brazil?" Sally knew the answer was Brasília. She raised her hand.

Mrs. Locati called on another person, and that's when Sally saw something familiar in the hallway. It was a lamp passing by — a lamp with socks hanging down.

It looked like *her* lamp, *her* socks.

Sally's face turned as white as a sheet, which is what fluttered by next.

"Oh," said Sally.

"Oh!" said Mrs. Locati, when the door burst open and an unmade bed fell in.

"Wow!" said the whole class, when a bureau crashed in on top of the bed, and a lamp came next, and play money and plastic horses bounced all over the floor.

Mrs. Locati stayed cool.

"People," she said,
"please take your seats.

As you can see, we
have a problem here."

And then she asked,
in a clear, calm voice,
"Just whose messy room is this?"

A couple of kids raised their hands, thinking it was their room,
but it was Sally who stood up and said,

"It's mine.

It's my room and I
like it that way.

I know where everything is."

"Yes," said the lamp. "It's your room, but you can't ever find anything."

"I can too," answered Sally.

"You couldn't find your sweater this morning," said the fishbowl.

The globe said, "You couldn't find your colored pencils, and you needed them for your map of South America."

Now Sally didn't know what to do. She stared out the window.

"Wait a second!" said the clock. "Look at Sally's desk!"

What a surprise!

Sally's desk was very tidy.
Her marker pens, workbooks, ruler, and pencils were all arranged carefully.
Her lunch was in the drawer.
There were no candy wrappers anywhere.

"I don't get it," said the lamp.

"How come, at school, people can be very neat
and know where everything goes,
but at home they
throw
things
around?"

"That's a good question!"
said Mrs. Locati.

Luckily for Sally, the
bell rang just then.

Sally rushed out the door.

Her room rushed out, too, but got hung up in the hallways.

Then it got stuck in afternoon traffic.

Sally arrived home first. She ran up the stairs, opened the door and, of course, there was nothing there.

"Gosh," she said. "What a big space.

I could draw huge pictures in here.

I could have all my friends over.

I could *dance* in here!"

Sally began to twirl and spin, graceful as a swan. She was a famous ballerina in a beautiful dress, dancing on the stage in front of everyone she knew,

until her room barged through the door and spread out all over the place.

And that was when Sally got a great idea, all by herself.

"Okay," she said.
"It is time for a change.

I have important things to do.
I need more *room* in this room."

The first thing Sally did was find a large box for toys and clothes to give away. She packed them carefully so that other children would like them.

"This game was fun when I was little," Sally thought, "but now it's boring."

Then she picked up all the underwear, socks, pajamas, shirts, shorts, skirts, pants, dresses, and blouses that needed washing. They went into a big laundry bag. Now she could see the floor again!

Sally cleaned the fishbowl
and fed the fish.
They liked it.

She arranged her horses and dolls on a
shelf where she could admire them.

She put her art supplies in one place so she could make drawings or clay monsters whenever she wanted. The books went into the bookcase. She gave the clock a battery.

She made the bed.
That's when she found her colored pencils.
That's when she found her favorite sweater.

As Sally put each thing away, the room began to feel big again.

It was a place where
anything
could happen.

Especially dancing!

When it was time for bed, Sally snuggled in her clean, soft sheets. She was tired.

"I still don't have a light bulb," said the lamp.

"Oh, well," answered the globe, "nobody's perfect."

Sally fell asleep that night in a very good mood.